The Time Train

'The Time Train'
An original concept by Jenny Jinks
© Jenny Jinks

Illustrated by Letizia Rizzo

Published by MAVERICK ARTS PUBLISHING LTD

Studio 3A, City Business Centre, 6 Brighton Road,

Horsham, West Sussex, RH13 5BB

© Maverick Arts Publishing Limited March 2019

+44 (0)1403 256941

A CIP catalogue record for this book is available at the British Library.

ISBN 978-1-84886-434-4

Maverick
publishing
www.maverickbooks.co.uk

White

This book is rated as: White Band (Guided Reading)

The Time Train

By Jenny Jinks

Illustrated by
Letizia Rizzo

Chapter 1

Astrid ran towards the station. She had to hurry. The train would be leaving any minute. As she turned the corner onto the platform, a huge, shiny, green steam train loomed into view.

"You made it!" a man said, appearing out of the steam. He was wearing a smart, old-fashioned conductor uniform, and had a twirly moustache that curled right up under his nose.

"Are you ready for the greatest adventure of all time?"

Astrid nodded excitedly.

"Then jump aboard!" he said, pulling out a gold pocket watch and blowing sharply on his whistle. Astrid hurried onto the train, just as it began to pull away.

The carriage was full of excited children. Astrid found a seat next to a girl with a camera. She was snapping pictures of everything.

"Hi," the girl said. "I'm Mia. Did you win a competition too?"

Astrid nodded. The ticket had arrived in the post with a letter saying that she had won a competition.

The funny thing was, Astrid didn't remember entering a competition. "Do you know where we're going?"

Mia shook her head, and they looked out of the window, but it was covered by thick white fog.

Mia chatted to Astrid the whole way.

They didn't even notice when the train stopped.

"Everybody off!" shouted the conductor.

"Where are we?" Mia asked, looking around.

They were in the middle of nowhere.

"You mean when are we!" said the conductor.

"Welcome to the Stone Age!"

Chapter 2

A long line of woolly mammoths came over.
CLICK! CLICK! went Mia's camera.

"Hop on," the conductor told the group. "Please
stay together. Don't change anything, or you
might change history."

Astrid and Mia climbed onto a mammoth with a boy called Jack.

"Say cheese!" said Mia, taking a picture of them all.

The mammoths plodded slowly off, past a huge hill that looked just like a dinosaur. CLICK! CLICK! went Mia's camera.

"This is boring," Jack said after a while. "Can't this thing go any faster?"

He nudged the mammoth. Suddenly it sped off, past rivers and trees, until the children couldn't hold on any longer. They landed with a bump, and the mammoth raced off.

"Oh no," said Astrid, looking around. There was no sign of the rest of the group. "We're lost, and we have no way to get back. We'll be stuck in the Stone Age forever!"

A strange man wandered out of a cave.

"Excuse me," Jack said. "Do you know the way back to the train?"

"Ug!" the man said, scratching his head.

"He doesn't understand. They didn't talk in the Stone Age," Mia said.

So Astrid drew a picture of the train on the cave wall. Ug still looked confused.

"He's probably never seen a train before," Mia said. "Hang on."

She grabbed her camera and showed Ug the picture of the dinosaur-shaped mountain. Ug looked at the camera in amazement. Then he took the stick and began drawing a map.

"We'll never make it that far on our own," Astrid said.

Mia showed Ug the photo of them all on the woolly mammoth. Ug scratched his head. Then he tipped his head back and shouted "Ugoooo! Ugooooo!"

Suddenly the ground began to rumble and shake. A huge cloud of dust came rushing towards them.

"Earthquake!" the children shouted.

The cloud of dust came skidding to a stop.

"Woolly rhinos?!" Jack said. "Cool!"

CLICK! CLICK! went Mia's camera.

"Come on, we'd better go," Astrid said.

They all climbed onto the rhinos, and they took off. If they thought riding a mammoth had been hard, it was nothing compared to a high speed woolly rhino! But riding the rhinos was much more fun. They were back at the dinosaur-shaped mountain in no time. And there was the train. Everyone else was just getting back too. Ug stared up at the train in amazement.

"Thanks, Ug," they said, climbing on board.

They watched the woolly rhinos chasing the train. Then a thick fog clouded the windows again, and they left the Stone Age behind them. But before long, the train stopped again.

"Everybody off," the conductor shouted.

"Are we home already?" Jack asked as they stepped off the train.

"This isn't home..." Astrid said, looking around.

"Welcome," said the conductor, "to Ancient Egypt."

Chapter 3

A line of camels was waiting to pick everyone up. But Astrid heard shouting nearby.

"I think someone's in trouble. Let's see what's going on," she said. "We'll catch up with the others later."

The friends crept closer and saw the Pharaoh yelling at a builder.

"NO! NO! NO!" the Pharaoh shouted, stomping

his foot. "You're fired!"

The builder ran away in floods of tears.

"You there!" the Pharaoh shouted to another builder. "Build me this!"

He thrust a bit of parchment at the builder. "No sir... we..."

"You're fired too!" He stormed off in a huff.

"He's rude, isn't he?" Mia muttered.

They wandered around the building site.

"They must be building the pyramids!" Mia said.

But nobody seemed to know what they were doing. They all looked miserable.

Then Astrid heard sniffing coming from behind a pile of stone.

"Not another upset builder," she said.

But to their surprise, it was the Pharaoh.

"All I wanted was a nice big triangle," the Pharaoh said. "Is that really too much to ask?"

"Well, you were a bit mean," Astrid said. "Maybe if you asked nicely?"

The Pharaoh sniffed and wiped his eye. "You really think that will work?"

"It's worth a try," Jack said.

Chapter 4

The builders looked terrified when they saw the Pharaoh coming.

"I'm sorry, sir. Your plan just doesn't work," a builder said.

"BUT WHY..." the Pharaoh shouted, then he stopped and took a deep breath. "Why didn't you just say so?" he asked, in his nicest voice.

"You wouldn't listen," the builder explained.

Astrid looked at the plans.

"Why don't you just build it the other way around?" she said, turning the drawing upside down.

The Pharaoh looked at the builder.

"That might work," the builder said.

"Excellent!" the Pharaoh boomed, making the builder jump. "What are you waiting for?"

The builder ran off before the pharaoh could start shouting again.

"How can I thank you?" the Pharaoh asked the children. "How about a ride on my camel?"

The children groaned. They had ridden enough animals for one day. Then they saw everyone getting back on the train.

"Sorry, got to go," Jack said quickly. They said goodbye and rushed back to the train.

"Home time," the conductor said as the train pulled into a station. The children got off and looked around. This was not home.

"Oh dear," the conductor said. "We've gone too far! We're in the future!"

Chapter 5

"Awesome!" Jack said.

"Don't go anywhere!" the conductor said.
"I will have the train fixed in no time."

But Mia wasn't listening. "Are you sure we're in
the future?" she said, looking disappointed.
"It doesn't look very different."

Then she saw a strange pod. "I wonder what
that does?" she said, wandering over and

looking inside. Astrid and Jack chased after her.

"Don't touch anything,"
Astrid warned her.
But Mia wasn't
listening. She pressed a
big red button.
They heard a PING!
But nothing happened.

"Boring, it doesn't even
do anything," Mia said.

They stepped back outside the pod. But they
weren't at the station any more. They had
appeared in the middle of a very busy city.

"We've teleported!"Astrid said.

"This is amazing!" Mia said.

There were flying cars, floating buildings, and robots rushing here and there. CLICK! CLICK! CLICK! went Mia's camera, taking about a million pictures. She wanted a photo of everything.

"Come on, we have to get back," Astrid said. She grabbed Mia's hand and pulled her back. But when they turned around, the pod was gone.

"Help! We're stuck here!" Astrid said in a
panic.

A robot suddenly appeared. "I am Help Bot.
Do you need help?"

"We need to get to the station," Astrid said.
"But the pod has... vanished!"

CLICK! CLICK! went Mia's camera.

"Follow me," said HelpBot, whizzing off down
the street. The children ran to keep up.
Finally they found another pod.

"Tele-Pod," said Help Bot. And then he disappeared as suddenly as he had arrived.

"What if it takes us to the wrong place?" Astrid said.

"What choice do we have?" Jack shrugged.

They all climbed inside. Mia pressed the big red button. **PING!** Jack peered outside.

"We made it!" he said. "We're back."

The friends climbed back on the train, tired and relieved. Finally the train came to a stop at the right station.

"Home at last," Astrid said.

"I hope we can go on the Time Train again soon," Jack said. "I wonder where else we could go?"

Then Astrid gasped. She pointed to a newspaper stand.

BREAKING NEWS: DID CAVEMEN INVENT TRAINS?

"My drawing!" Astrid groaned. "The conductor warned us not to change anything!"

"Don't worry," Jack said. "I'm sure we can't have caused any real trouble."

The End

Book Bands for Guided Reading

The Institute of Education book banding system is a scale of colours that reflects the various levels of reading difficulty. The bands are assigned by taking into account the content, the language style, the layout and phonics. Word, phrase and sentence level work is also taken into consideration.

Maverick Early Readers are a bright, attractive range of books covering the pink to white bands. All of these books have been book banded for guided reading to the industry standard and edited by a leading educational consultant.

Pink
Red
Yellow
Blue
Green
Orange
Turquoise
Purple
Gold
White

To view the whole Maverick Readers scheme, visit our website at
www.maverickearlyreaders.com

Or scan the QR code above to view our scheme instantly!